W9-CDN-270

To my late great friend Robert O'Keefe.
— Adam Ciccio

To my superheroes Olivia, Anatole, and Capucine.
— Emmanuel Volant

Originally published as *De oranje cape* in Belgium and the Netherlands by Clavis Uitgeverij, 2020

Visit us on the Web at www.clavis-publishing.com.

The Boy in the Orange Cape written by Adam Ciccio and illustrated by Emmanuel Volant

ISBN 978-1-60537-599-1

This book was printed in December 2020 at Nikara, M. R. Štefánika 858/25, 963 01 Krupina, Slovakia.

First Edition
10 9 8 7 6 5 4 3 2 1

Clavis Publishing supports the First Amendment and celebrates the right to read.

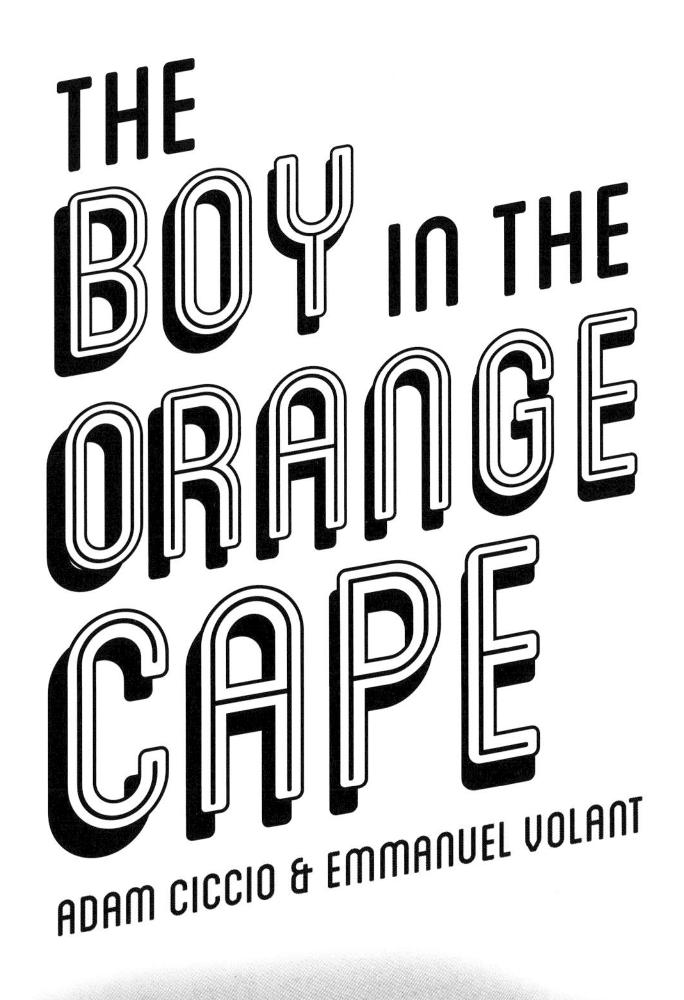
THE
BOY IN THE
ORANGE
CAPE
ADAM CICCIO & EMMANUEL VOLANT

SCHOOL BUS
2452018

Clavis

NEW YORK

I'll tell you this story, because it may help you one day.

It begins with a boy who wore an **ORANGE CAPE** to school every single day.
The brave young boy's name was **Corey.**
And **Corey** stuck out like a sore thumb.

SCHOOL
BUS
STOP

All the kids stared at him. They thought he was weird,
and called his **ORANGE CAPE** silly.
Billy, the school's biggest bully, thought **Corey**
and his **CAPE** were absurd. So what did Billy do?
He followed **Corey** around and ripped his **CAPE** right off.

SCHOOL
BUS
STOP

Every day, Billy took **Corey's** cape.
And every day, **Corey** came back to school with a **NEW CAPE,** even though he knew that Billy would just take it again. And again. And again.

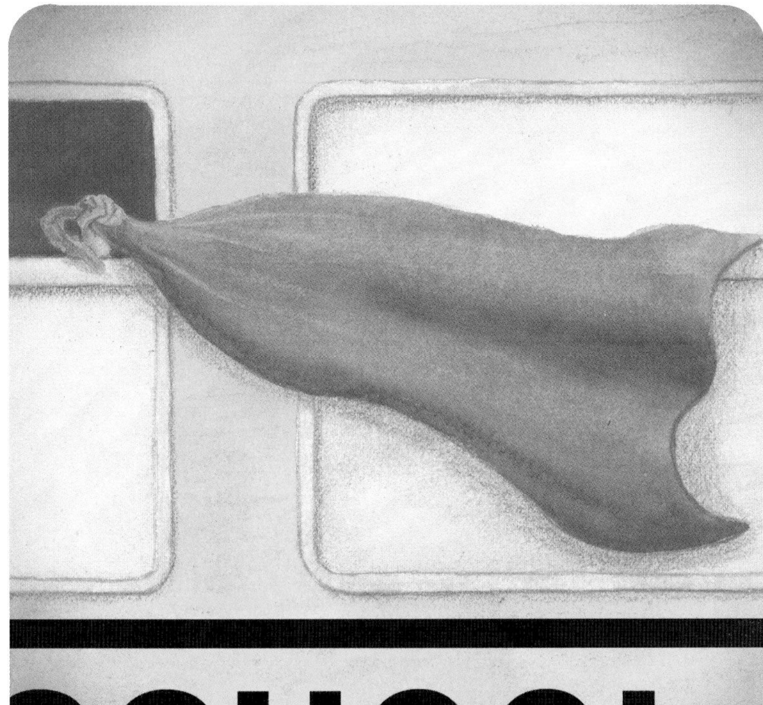
SCHOOL

The other kids noticed the bullying, but no one was brave enough to confront Billy, and no one would dare be seen with **Corey.** Until one boy got curious.

"If you know he's going to take it, why do you keep wearing that **SILLY CAPE?**" the boy asked.
"My mom is sick," **Corey** explained. "I wear this **CAPE** to support her. And it's orange, because orange is her favorite color. That way, she knows I think about her."
"That's *really* cool," the curious boy said.

The next day, the school bus stopped for the curious boy and **Corey** couldn't believe his eyes. The boy was wearing a **STRIPED CAPE!**

SCHOOL

The story of **Corey's** **CAPE** had spread around quickly.
As the bus continued, he saw a **RED CAPE.**

Then he saw a **POLKA DOT CAPE.**

And a **CAPE IN THE SHAPE OF A UNICORN.**

Some boys wore a baseball cap . . .
and a **PINK CAPE.**

Some girls wore a **POLKA DOT CAPE,** others a **STRIPED ONE.**

And others wore **CAPES IN DIFFERENT COLORS.**

All of the girls wore a **CAPE!** All of the boys!
Except Billy.

The playground was a sea of **COLORFUL CAPES,** except where Billy was.
Now it was Billy who stuck out like a sore thumb.
Now Billy felt weird, and was called silly.

Corey walked up to him and pulled another orange cape out of his bag. "This one's for you," **Corey** said. "It's one of my **OLD CAPES.** I've managed to save a few."

Billy thanked **Corey** and smiled carefully.
"Thank you," he said. "And . . . I'm sorry."

From that day on, Billy wore an **ORANGE CAPE** too.
Because orange was **Corey's** favorite color.